I0718193

DEPTHS OF THE HEART

STEPHANIE FLYNN

Small Fish Publishing

Small Fish Publishing

USA

This is a work of fiction. Names, characters, places, and incidents either are the products of the author's imagination or are used fictitiously. Any resemblance to actual persons, living or dead, businesses, companies, events, or locales is entirely coincidental.

Copyright © 2023 Stephanie Flynn

All rights reserved. This book or parts thereof may not be reproduced in any form, stored in any retrieval system, or transmitted in any form by any means—electronic, mechanical, photocopy, recording, or otherwise.

First edition
Cover design by Stephanie Flynn
ISBN eBook: 9781952372445
ISBN paperback: 9781952372865

Also By Stephanie Flynn

Find my catalog at StephanieFlynn.com

Immortal Protector series
0.5 Vampire's Distraction
1 Vampire's Deception
2 Vampire's Secret
3 Vampire's Promise
3.5 Elf Bound
4 Vampire's Demand
5 Vampire's Destruction
6 Vampire's Conquest

Immortal Protector Side Tales
Deer Holiday

Love Claws
Depths of the Heart

Matchmaker in Time series
0.5 Minutes to Live
1 Seconds to Act
2 Hours to Arrive
3 Days to Hide
4 Years to Savor

Pirates in Time series
1 Pirate's Prize
2 Pirate's Treasure
3 Pirate's Plunder

Time Travel Romance Shorts
Fateful Time
One Crazy Time

If you like your urban fantasy without the romance, too, check out Stephanie Flynn's other name, Marie Flynn!

Forbidden Fruit

THOSE OF US PREPARED for the impending storm's fury sat at the bar. Some of us fed a pleasant buzz to distract from the inevitable repair work, while others impatiently waited for the danger to pass. Sitting beside my sister, Adria, I was neither. I sipped from my ale while exchanging glances across the bar. A group of sailors taking refuge boisterously regaled tales of the sea, relishing the shore leave. Thumps of mugs splashed ale on the bar inside the smokey tavern, aptly named Pirate's Cove, while others voiced concern over their shipmates still out there.

Across the cobblestone road where waves clawed at the breakwater, brave sailors aloft in the rigging scrambled to tie wayward sails in place. I couldn't imagine life aboard those ships. From this vantage point, overlooking the angry sea, I wouldn't want to fight this storm or any other, risking everything I owned and loved to the whims of Mother Nature. This storm was a ship-killer, and time was running low for those poor souls scrambling in the cove.

Just like them, only granules of sand remained in my hourglass. Soon I would be dragged back to my duty—a thought requiring the strongest of buzzes from the dredges of the bartender's lowest barrel. Except not tonight. Someone special across the bar was all the distraction I needed. I wasn't permitted to stretch my legs all that often, so until that last granule tumbled down, I kept quiet.

And a close flirty watch.

In the sea of sailors filling the tight space, a handsome human on the other end of the bar sent me long stretches of eye contact and sly lifts of his lips. With a carefully obscured smile of my own, I met his piercing green eyes that knew depths of the world I could only dream. I would never forget his crooked nose, leaving me to wonder about the cause—fights won or lost? And neatly trimmed, dark hair dusted a strong jaw. Whenever he attempted to approach me—both tonight and on a previous serendipitous occasion, one of his sailors interfered, redirecting the handsome human's attention to where it belonged. Unfamiliar with human nuances I knew not the dangers he faced, but I knew mine, and I should heed them.

But the folk I lived with hardly ever smiled, and the stories weren't boisterous, entertaining, or as fascinating. What would it be like to remain ashore, to cast aside this life I'd been sold into? Perhaps even staying with a certain human someone?

My handsome sailor winked at me, and I sipped ale to shield my lips from the dutiful and proud sister sitting at my elbow. Silly dreams didn't come true in my world, but I could still dream. No one could take that from me, unlike my freedom.

"Cali, the ale tastes off since the last time we were here. Don't you think so?" Adria asked, frowning at her drink. Bushy brown hair nested above her beautiful face with sharp eyes and a dainty nose. For a while, I believed the handsome sailor's attention was directed at her, but no. It was me he wanted.

"Oh, yes. Definitely," I said, absentmindedly catching another sneaky glance at my distracted sailor.

All night tonight, I yearned to introduce myself. So why not go to him?

Adria.

And the forbidden rules of our secret world.

The coveted Salvage Squad—an organization that pilfered sunken treasures from capsized vessels—had issued a request recently for a new member, and my parents eagerly sold me for the honor. The retrieval of lost human goods didn't bother me; in fact, I beamed with pride in completing my tasks, but had I known the dark truth of what lurked within the soul of the organization, I would've fled home rather than live by a code I never accepted and couldn't escape.

And, as far as I knew, I was the only mermaid shifter to struggle with these traitorous thoughts, which I carefully kept hidden from Adria. The handsome human winking at me from across the bar stirred a dangerous level of yearning for an impossible future.

A human and a mermaid? A youngling's fairy tale.

A mermaid escaping the Salvage Squad? The thought alone could lead to death, which was why I enjoyed toying with the fairy tale before me, but I still begrudgingly followed my sister's orders—no matter how depraved they were.

Honor in Duty

I NEVER UNDERSTOOD HOW humans could eat animal flesh. And since I'd witnessed the occasion at Pirate's Cove so infrequently, I never gave it much thought. Growing up, I'd tended my family's seagrass garden with my pitchfork, which I wielded against those blasted manatees. But I never harmed them, only attempted to ward off those endless eating machines. When I'd been conscripted into the Salvage Squad, my boss had...unique tastes, and when I'd learned we were all required to participate, that curiosity had returned. I had guessed various sea vertebrates were behind the unpleasant menu, but I'd been wrong. The chewy texture belonged to two-legged creatures of the land variety. After the sea softened the skin and turned the organs to soup, the tender meat would be eaten off the bone, like humans did to cooked animals. My revulsion nearly boiled over, but I maintained my composure and found ways to avoid that duty.

There was one distinct and important difference between the diet of humans and that of the Salvage Squad. Humans mingling with their food posed no threat to them, while mermaids mingling with smart, fearless hunters was incredibly dangerous. So unless I lured a human below the sea to the dinner table for the Squad, socializing was forbidden.

I caught another wistful glance at the handsome sailor. The pairing of a human and a mermaid was simply a fairy tale.

"Cali?"

A gust of wind snuffed the candles by the door. The fearsome storm arrived.

"Calista!"

Tearing my gaze from the handsome sailor, I answered, "What?"

"Oi, storm's a'comin', and I'm closin' up The Cove. Get out while you can!" the bartender shouted over Mother Nature's fury and the boisterous humans within.

Groans of displeasure and the rattle of metal accompanied men picking up their personal effects, dropping coins on the bar, and shuffling out the door to find other accommodations willing to brave the storm. Those giving up the search would return to their rocking vessels, but tender boats were no match for the swells approaching.

Easy targets.

"We need to leave," Adria said.

"Yeah," I said absently. The handsome sailor approached, flanked by his crew. On his belt hung a cutlass and a dagger, and cuffed leather boots reached his knees. His piercing green eyes darted my way. Armed, strong, and beautiful. I feared I'd never see him again. Unable to help myself, I bumped a few pieces of eight off the bar. They tinkled against the wood floor.

The handsome sailor was the only man to stop. He bent down and collected them with thick, strong fingers. As he rose, I caught a whiff of his scent, a familiar salty sweat but with a tinge of something foreign, exotic, captivating.

So close, yet so far away.

"Miss, you dropped these." He held them out between a pinch of his fingers.

"Oh, clumsy me." I opened my palm, and he gently set them down and closed my fingers over them. His touch—rough and commanding, yet gentle and delicate—sent my heart pounding. "Thank you."

"Anytime." He tipped his hat and grinned.

"Let's go!" One of his mates captured his arm and dragged him away.

I didn't want this short exchange to be over so soon. "Be safe out there," I called to his departing back.

The sailor turned and winked.

Tell me your name! I silently pleaded.

"It's hard to separate the mark from his pack," Adria said. "You'll get it one of these times."

I cleared my throat and peeled my attention away. What Adria thought I'd planned for the handsome sailor was nothing she'd approve of, so I played along. "I only offered a platitude, so maybe next time, I'll succeed, but the odds are these men will try their luck with Poseidon's playground tonight."

Adria deviously grinned. "I like your thinking. We need good news and a good storm because I'm starving." Adria tapped the bar where she'd left her payment.

With a sigh, I reluctantly added the coins the handsome sailor placed in my palm to the pile.

"Come now before the boss gets upset."

I dutifully strolled outside with my sister, catching sly glances over my shoulder up and down the walkway for the handsome sailor, but no such luck. I hoped he found formidable accommodations tonight. Maybe next time we visit the human town, I'd see him again.

Across the cobblestone road, at the sea's edge, we stopped. Ocean water misted my face, and the growing wind tossed my tangled hair.

"Look, there." Adria pointed offshore.

Under the angry dark skies and vicious swells, a vessel anchoring outside the bay struggled, listing severely against the fearsome waves, and sure enough, a tender rowed uselessly against the mighty sea.

Foolish humans.

"Looks like Poseidon's rewarding us with a meal *and* some treasure. The boss will be pleased, and I should think we'll be handsomely rewarded. Come now. Duty calls." Adria rubbed her hands together with anticipation and dove under the next wave.

I wished for a *handsome* reward, but not how Adria imagined. I shifted my weight, relishing in the last few moments with my legs—feeling the cool of the sand, the tickle of the breeze—before the magic of the sea stripped them away. I turned, facing the tavern. The lights had been snuffed and the doors closed. My duty weighed on me, but the urge to find that handsome man was powerful. I couldn't pound on doors asking for a man I had no name for.

With a sigh of resignation, I dove into the cool, salty water. I kicked to descend, and moments later, my legs fused as the scaled tail took its place below my hips. Gills opened, allowing me breath, and I zipped through the water like a bird on the breeze, leaving my garments to drift away. The men rowing the tender had no idea what fate awaited them. I cringed on their behalf.

Storm of Serendipity

ABOVE THE SURFACE, POWERFUL winds carried deafening rain, but down here, the sea hampered the noise. The raucous storm became a murmur of rolling thunder beneath. My inhuman vision allowed me perfect sight through the murky depths. I soared through the undulating waters, heading toward my sister, who hovered in place, neck craned up toward the surface. I cautiously approached her side. Oars from a tender boat rhythmically stabbed at the fearsome sea, paddling like a panicking sea monster. Men shouted encouragement to continue their plight, only a murmur reaching my ears.

While studying the tender, Adria asked, "What caused your delay?"

Suspicion was dangerous. I needed a distraction, something to ease the worrisome thoughts in her obedient mind. I craned my neck up to the passing boat. The men shouted again. The rail of the tender breached the surface. Water spilled into the hull, further listing the tiny vessel into the demanding sea. Those men above were at grave risk. Foolish! They were fools for toiling in the sea tonight, and there was nothing I could do to change their course. Their fates were in Poseidon's hands now. "You were right, Adria. The tender will bring food to the table tonight."

Adria shifted her attention. "We don't receive such generous offerings frequently. Ready yourself for the quick task."

I smiled at my successful redirection but wanted to frown at the schooling. I'd retrieved drowned sailors before. I knew how to do my job. My willingness, however, required her lecture, but Adria could never discover it.

The men's boots splashed in the sinking boat; the pounding movements filled with panic. The rail listed sharply once more, and oars spilled over and sank, like a white flag of surrender. With shouts, men toppled into the water. For reasons I couldn't explain, so many sailors never learned to swim.

And I thought my occupation was hazardous.

Sailors kicked their boots, but with their personal effects weighing them down, even those who could swim struggled. Adria delegated the tasks at hand. "I'm getting this one. You get that one. When these two are ready for the boss, we'll return for the rest. They'll squirm far less by then."

Less? Being dead, the sailors wouldn't squirm at all. And imagining the greedy face on my boss as she chewed on their meaty bones with a hearty appetite, my stomach twisted with bile. To me, that was worse than death.

Tasted awful, too.

I swallowed back those dreadful thoughts and nodded my understanding. Guilt weighed heavily on my shoulders, an effect more obvious on the surface, but ever present down here. I swam to my charge and scooped him by the arms to slow his descent. Before delivering him as ordered, I brushed the man's billowing hair out of his face. My eyes widened in recognition—my handsome man from Pirate's Cove. His panicked mouth opened, and air bubbles escaped. I didn't need to know what he said to understand him.

Help! Please, help me.

On land, humans roamed fearsome, mighty, and prepared, but under the sea was merfolk territory. Humans stood no chance against their finned counterparts. To return to the Salvage Squad empty-handed was a common occurrence, but this time Adria knew I had food to deliver. I could never excuse losing a human, and to do so risked my life.

It was his life or mine.

The handsome sailor thrashed for the surface, but his weaponry, boots, and heavy coat dragged him down. He would drown. There was no question of it.

I glanced at the terrified green eyes of the one human who allowed my whimsical daydreams of a fairy tale nature. A gift he didn't know he gave. Then I pictured myself chewing on his bones, following orders like always, while silently stewing in disgust and hatred for myself. What would he think of my cowardice?

The handsome sailor's hand gripped my shoulder in desperation to return to the surface. More bubbles released, and not many remained. Something about those kind eyes of his called to me, in a different way than I'd ever known before. In the face of my sisters and boss, could I tear off a bite of his flesh with my own teeth and stomach it? Could I hide my disgust and hatred any longer?

More importantly, could I trust this human with my life?

The Decision

In that moment, despite all the trouble my choice would bring, the answer was clear. I would figure out how to cover my decision later, but for now, the handsome sailor was running out of time. Without another second's hesitation, I soared through the water like a starving shark to bait, hoping the pressure of my speed wasn't too much for him, but if I went slower, he would drown. I carried the man to the shallows near an isolated shore, not far from the tavern. I suspected this was far enough Adria wouldn't catch me right away.

Waist-deep in water, I settled him on his feet. He tipped over, and I steadied his footing. He coughed and gasped. Water ran down his face covered with hair. Without my legs, I tread water while the human towered over me. The rain pounded hard, and he swiped water out of his eyes and pushed back his hair. He coughed again. The handsome man was alive, just as I wanted, but now I had to leave. To be spotted with my tail was forbidden just like conversing with a human, and I'd already broken enough rules for one night. I had other men to collect on Adria's orders, but I couldn't force myself to go just yet.

The human smiled at me, and my heart pounded in my chest—a foreign feeling I very much liked.

"Thank you for saving my life, miss. How shall I ever repay you?"

I returned the contagious smile, excited to finally meet him. "Tell me your name."

"Jack Roberts." He held out his hand, but I didn't know why. "Now it's your turn. What's the name of my beautiful rescuer?"

To tell him would attach a name to the story—an affirmation of my guilt and a witness to my treason. But I couldn't help myself from connecting with this human. I wanted him to know. "Calista."

Jack tilted his head as he studied me, hand still hanging in the air. "Correct me if I'm mistaken, but you are the beauty from Pirate's Cove. Give me your hand so I may properly thank you, Calista."

My name on his tongue rolled through my body like how I'd imagined the caress of a lover's touch. I offered my hand out of the water.

Jack's touch sent my heart skipping. He leaned down and kissed my knuckles. Flitting butterflies in my stomach made me pull from his grasp in surprise. But I wanted more. I wanted to know what those lips felt like on the rest of my body.

"The crew who survived the plunge of our tender would've returned to shore. We can meet up with them and dry off. Come with me, and I'll buy you a proper drink."

A thrill of exhilaration warmed my cool bones. He'd invited me to what I'd dreamed of—an escape from the Salvage Squad and the depths of the sea—but I couldn't. "I'm afraid I must decline."

With a gentle lift of his lips, Jack said, "You must be chilled. The waves will wash you back out to sea, and I can't go in after you. You must regale me with how you learned to swim so well, so incredibly fast."

I had watched humans whenever the opportunity arose, but I never met one so kind, and he was a little amusing, too. I'd risked enough simply by saving his life and offering my name. My tail needed to dry before it would magically stow away for later use, and in this pelting storm, dry wasn't possible before Jack saw what I was. "I'm sorry. I wish I could."

His disappointment squeezed my chest like a suffocating blanket, and before Jack could convince me otherwise, I turned away and dove into the waves, tail flicking as I sped away from temptation.

At the wreck site of the tender, Adria was collecting a drowned sailor from the ocean bed. Before my sister spotted my failure, I darted toward the last body and scooped him into my arms. He'd already passed, but still, my duty was no easier for it. Swallowing down deep sorrow, and unable to face my sister, I quickly put distance between me and Adria.

Dark Task

I was new to the Squad. My sister Adria, my mentor, explained many of our required tasks and the schedule rotation. This was one I hadn't yet done and hoped to avoid entirely. Whenever Poseidon gifted us a bounty, we had to store much of it for later use, and Jack's floundering tender boat was no exception. Despite the caloric burn from our underwater labors and the endless appetite of our boss, a group of mermaids couldn't eat an entire pack of men at once. Today, of all days, I was assigned the task. My stomach knotted more than ever before, but I wasn't sure if facing my sisters after what I'd done would've been any easier.

Jack's rescue hadn't raised any suspicion, but I couldn't risk any further disobedience. Reluctantly, I went to work. In the underwater cave, lit only by a crevice in the high roof, the gentle waters allowed the ocean to work its magic without damage to the meat. Chaining the bodies in place was useless, as limbs tended to separate themselves over time. I grimaced as I repositioned one body next to the other, avoiding the vacant pale gaze of the deceased judging me. These were Jack's friends. This could've been Jack. I had to brush away that visual before I broke down in sobs of what could've been.

A lifeless hand brushed my shoulder. Having been stripped of all his possessions and most of his clothing, I touched his bare wrist and glanced at his face, for a second forgetting he was gone.

"I'm sorry. I wish I could've saved you."

I met his vacant gaze—long hair billowed around his bearded face. The lines once pronounced on shore were softened. He appeared to be in his forties, a sailor with vast experience, and this was how he ended. A waste of a life—not because of his choices that brought him here, but because he could've been rescued. Had Adria and I returned the spilled men to their tender or even delivered them to their vessel, he would still be breathing. All of them would be.

I met each of their same lifeless gazes. They could no longer voice their opinions or their dreams. Did they have families waiting for them? Jack Roberts was alive, waiting for them. Was he fighting the storm alone on the street searching, or was he...drowning...his sorrows over these men in a tavern willing to brave the storm? Tears sprung to my eyes. Neither of those possibilities brought me hope that my actions had meant something to him.

Honor or not, I couldn't live like this. I pressed my palm against Jack's friend's chest. "Your sacrifice won't be for nothing. I promise you this."

With my task complete, I swam to the outside of the cave and carefully shifted the barricade in place. Sharks would sniff them out, and since I was already toeing the line of punishment, I had to protect the food supply. Besides, there was nothing I could do for them now.

"Calista, there you are." Adria appeared.

I almost cried out in fright. My sister used my full name, which meant I was in trouble. Sheepishly, feeling the warmth spring to my cheeks, I asked, "What brings you down here?"

Adria's eyes shifted to the cave door. "When you first arrived, the boss raised suspicions about you. At the time, I refused to entertain such wild ideas—look at you—your parents begged us to take you. They accepted a measly hundred clams for you. I thought that meant you'd be grateful for your family's rise. Instead, your unwillingness only deepened. Despite my staunch position of your obedience, doubt crept along until I could no longer ignore her words."

None of that boded well for me. "I don't understand."

"I counted the drowned sailors. We're missing one."

My heart thundered in my chest, a completely different feeling from when Jack kissed my knuckles. "Are you sure?"

My sister swam up to my face, closing the distance, anger twisting her features. "Where's the missing sailor, Cali?"

In the face of accusation, the urge to relieve the burdensome guilt filled every limb of my body, but I didn't want to die for saving Jack's life. Overreacting was damning evidence, and plausible deniability was all I had left. I calmly said, "I don't know what you're talking about.

I didn't keep track of how many drowned. Are you sure the missing one didn't come to his senses and swim to shore?"

Adria glared as if trying to see the truth written on the backs of my eyeballs.

I swallowed thickly and glanced away, not regretting for a second what I'd done, and come what may, I'd do it all over again a thousand times over.

Adria sniffed haughtily. "You're my sister, so I'm offering you one consolation."

Like she intended to stick her neck out for me? I was certainly surprised at this turn from her. "Like what?"

"A head start."

My belly twisted. "A what?"

The disappointment was palpable on Adria's tone. "As soon as I return to the organization, the boss will send us out to hunt you. It pains me to see you on the wrong side of our team, especially since you aren't the first."

Curiosity got the better of me. "What happened to her?"

"She was dinner." Adria's pointed stare was enough.

If I was next on the table, I couldn't do anything to make those men's sacrifices mean anything. And with the Squad's abundant experience, I stood no chance against them all. Internally thanking my sister for the gift of time, however short it might be, I fled.

Drawn to the Fruit

I swam harder and faster than ever before, zipping through the dark waters as if being chased by a hungry shark, but I was hunted by worse. A shark could be outsmarted. I could stay low, thwarting its natural hunting pattern. I could fit inside places it couldn't, and eventually it would give up the wait. If sharks were frightening predators, merfolk were terrifying sea monsters. My kind used strategy, weapons, and vast numbers like an army to do their bidding. The most crucial being to protect the merfolk from discovery after humans believed us to be extinct hundreds of years ago. To maintain our invisibility, merfolk were cunning, patient, and most terrifying of all: ruthless.

And I'd just betrayed them all to save the life of our enemy.

I couldn't return to the Squad, not that I

ever wanted to be there in the first place. Would Adria receive punishment for aiding my escape? I doubted it. My sister was capable of protecting herself, and since she and the boss were of the same mind, Adria would at most receive a tongue-lashing. More likely, she'd just lie. In the meantime, the Squad would send a pair to search for me at my old comfort locations—my parents' cave, the community gardens, or the local meeting clubs, where eligible merfolk mingled to mate. I couldn't consider going anywhere near any of those places, but I also had nowhere else to go. Despite what would come for me, I still had no regrets.

I let my fins take me away from the imminent threat. At some point, I'd have to make a deliberate plan to find a new home. The various merfolk clans were testy about territory. Finding human-free homes were difficult, so when a safe area had been discovered, merfolk were, well, ruthless. I wasn't strong enough to claim my own land, so I'd have to find a clan willing to take in a stranger. There would be questions, distrust, and unease. Why would I leave my clan? If I hadn't, then what had I done to be exiled? If for no other reason than curiosity, they'd send a messenger to ask my clan, and I would be outed as a traitor in my new home at once. Back to the seas alone I would flee.

Just as I was right now.

I finally noticed the unusual quiet above. I surfaced. The raging storm had receded, leaving behind grumpy waves and dull gray skies. Pirate's Cove had survived, but the candles remained extinguished, and no patrons entered or left. The threatened vessel in the bay, the one Jack's tender fought to reach, which had listed dangerously in the storm, had survived. Its crew rushed along the deck to prepare for something important. I couldn't fare to guess, but I enjoyed watching them. From their stories in the Cove, I waited for the song as they worked, wanting something uplifting for my spirits as dreary as this day.

An arm reached over the rail, pointing down at me. "Man overboard!" a deep voice bellowed into the air.

Before I could swim away, and before I could decide if I wanted to, another man leaped over the rail. Wearing knee high boots over loose breeches, an ivory tunic, and a bright sash free of weapons, he climbed down the footholds with impressive speed. Curiosity had me watching his movements, so fluid on his human feet. He leaned toward me, urging me to reach for his hand.

I gazed at the familiar face in wonder—the very same Jack Roberts.

Recognition dawned on him. "Calista? Come to me. Hurry now!"

Humans were food. They were to be feared. I'd been raised, instructed, and reminded to follow the rules of my world. I irreparably broke the direst—contacting humans and thereby risking the merfolk world. For if humans discovered our existence, the humans would turn their whaling vessels into merfolk vessels once again.

But I hadn't seen the evils of the human ways. Instead, it was my own kind who hunted me. Going home and pleading for mercy was no longer an option. As Adria had explained, I would be served on the dinner table, just like the last traitor.

I could flee—swim the depths of the ocean alone, hunting for a new merfolk clan that would embrace my desires to live as I once knew and never raise suspicions about my past. That impossibility only reinforced how much I didn't belong here.

But if I accepted Jack's offer, he and his crew would discover what I was.

Dangerous Choice

Blind to the real world around them, all younglings trusted their families. Ever since the day my parents excitedly announced an opening in the Squad and insisted I apply, trust had been on shaky grounds. Against my wishes, my parents sold me, and I'd been heartbroken. When the Salvage Squad revealed its depravity, I'd been disgusted. And after seeing how Adria aligned herself with the boss, I couldn't trust my own sister, my mentor, either. Down here, that title meant she was on equal footing with family. I now realize how deep that equality had embedded itself, and it was no longer reassuring.

Jack—a stranger from a strange world, a human on a ship full of predators, enemies—wanted me to join him. No longer capable of trusting my own kind's endless messages warning us of humanity's threat,

I could only judge a human by what I'd witnessed. While avoiding Adria's suspicions and enjoying the warm gazes from Jack, I'd listened to the crew's tales at the Pirate's Cove—boisterous and full of laughter. I heard not a word of cruelty, only harmless fun.

But I'd seen enough boats hauling nets full of fish to hesitate. Would they see me differently from other finned creatures? Jack was kind to me, but he didn't know my secret. Could I trust all of these humans with my life?

Gentle waves lapped at the hull, a steady musical rhythm, brushing me closer to Jack. A seagull cawed as it soared through the rigging, as if pleading with me to just take his hand. Was Mother Nature guiding my choice? Was Poseidon urging me to choose a new life?

Jack waited patiently, wearing a beaming grin that suited him well. His excitement was palpable. Inhaling deeply, lost in those sparkling green eyes of his, I took his hand, and when our skin touched, it was just like the first time, tingles of heat and flutters of my heart. He pulled me close, and my breath hitched. Nerves fluttered through my stomach. I wanted to kiss him, but I hesitated. "Wait."

Jack's lips met my knuckles. "I've waited a lifetime for a woman so amazing as you. If I must wait a moment longer, I fear I'll explode. Come, let me get you fed and dry."

I resisted his tug and gestured toward the crew above. "What about them? Will they be kind to me, like you are?"

Jack rubbed my hand in comfort. "Rest assured, my lady. By my orders, they won't harm you."

That simple promise seemed too good to be true, and I wanted so desperately to believe his words, but the stories from my parents, hammering home the dangers of humans, echoed in my memory. So ingrained the scaremongering, I struggled to see through it. I cocked a brow at him. "You're certain?"

"These sea dogs had their fill of shore leave. Since you saved my life, they agreed to grant you clemency from their barbaric urges." His tone was light and friendly. Almost playful. Jack had already told the crew about me, but he missed one key detail.

Unable to stomach a life alone, hunted by my own kind, I had to be sure Jack could handle my secret before I could accept his offer. "I have something to show you. Please don't be alarmed."

Jack waited, patient as ever, and I twisted my hips, tail fin breaching the surface. His grip on my hand never faltered, but I was prepared to flee if necessary. I studied Jack's reaction.

He sent me a crooked smile, and my heart thumped wildly. "They're more beautiful when you move slower."

I gasped. "You knew?"

Jack nodded and pulled my hand to the hull, bringing my face close to his. Salty sweat filled my nose, and I yearned to touch him. I swished my tail to remain high enough out of the water so Jack didn't strain.

"It's hard to miss such shimmering beauty above the vicious waves. Don't mind my men. They all know, and what I promised keeps them motivated for the account at hand."

The account. I'd heard the term before. Images flitted through my mind of a merfolk vessel outfitted with spears and nets. Horror seized me as the images worsened—of men eagerly hauling merfolk aboard and chomping greedily on our flesh through the screams and protests. Jack's grip on my hand was almost painful. I swallowed back the tremble in my voice. "Are you going to eat me?"

Jack chuckled, a deep rumble in his chest. "Are you going to eat *me*?"

His silly response, so light and playful, relaxed me. I rapidly shook my head. No way. Never again.

Something touched my tail fin. Before I could react, a tight grip yanked me below the surface. Since Jack grasped my hand, he went with me. The current of the ocean and the unexpected force stole Jack from my grip.

Caught

A COLD HAND FASTENED onto my wrist, and immediately I knew it wasn't Jack's. I tried to free myself with a quick tug, but it was useless. One of the Squad members—one I'd never been friendly with—gripped me with an impossible strength. She would not be an ally. Trembling, I followed her gaze to my boss—a thick woman with a broad tail, and short hair drifting around the scowl on her lined face. She held her shoulders square and her hands clasped behind her back. A terror in the flesh.

I searched the mermaids flanking my boss for spears...or forks. Adria waited for orders at the boss's side, and several others from the Salvage Squad fanned out behind them, frowning, arms crossed in displeasure, ready to obey. The Squad was impatient, but I truly thought I had more time.

I brought this fight on myself, but Jack didn't

deserve this. Where was he? Air bubbles and frantic thrashing had me craning my neck. A pair of mermaids pinned the human between them. Jack uselessly clawed at his captors' hands while bubbles of panic escaped his lips.

At the heart-rending sight, I knew at once what I desired. Jack was the only person who showed me kindness, something I would forever be grateful for. Swallowing back the meek mermaid silently stewing on her disobedience, I remembered my promised to his drowned friends. They would not die in vain, and neither would Jack. I would fight for those who treated me fairly, not the ones who continued to force me to do their bidding. The odds didn't matter. I had to stand for what I believed in. I had to save the human. I lifted my chin, ready to take them all on. "Let him go!"

They didn't.

The boss approached me with a calm menace. "You expect me to obey orders from you, Calista? I have to admit, I'm surprised."

The boss paced, shoulders squared and hair billowing out of her face. Amusement played on her lips, and that was more terrifying than anger. Despite my curiosity, I said nothing.

"I usually offer a bribe when I want a particular apprentice, but your parents were so desperate and pathetic, pleading with me. They insisted you could be molded. See, I could work with that. To close the deal—that I didn't want—your parents accepted half the normal bribe. I expected you to follow in their footsteps, making you useless to me. And now here we are. You broke rank and disobeyed orders. You allowed our food to get away. You exposed us to the humans. And now you have *feelings* for this one?" The boss scoffed. "You are a disgrace, an embarrassment to merfolk across the seas."

She wasn't wrong, but instead of tears of shame, I met her scowl with one of my own. Jack was innocent, and he wouldn't survive much longer, but not for a moment did I consider pleading for mercy. No, the boss knew no mercy, but I could be certain the dire consequences would befall on me and only me. For the short while it lasted, this human had freed me from a wretched life of chains. I was grateful beyond measure, but I had yet to thank him. Hopefully, he'd forgive me for not getting the chance. I squared my shoulders to meet hers. "Let the human go free, and I'll take my punishment as you see fit."

The hulls of longboats breached the surface by Jack's vessel, and oars stabbed at the sea. The boss paid them no mind, but those humans were up to something. I could only hope they planned to help Jack. He was going to need it.

"You're in no position to bargain." The boss gestured. "Ladies, take them both away."

"Come on, Cali," Adria said, reaching for me.

"No!" I shouted as her hands fastened to my arms. "Adria, please!" My plea wasn't for myself, but for Jack's forgiveness. He was terrified, confused, and running out of time.

Spears struck the sea and barreled down like diving birds, and one impaled the boss's shoulder. Her mouth gaped with shock as the force dragged her down to the dark depths. In a flurry of panic, the mermaids released Jack, and micro bubbles escaped his calm lips. He didn't thrash, and he didn't panic. Hair gently drifted around his head, covering his beautiful face as he sunk.

I wasn't too late. I refused to believe the humans were too late to save him.

More spears rained down upon us, catching some mermaids fatally, while others took flesh wounds. The Salvage Squad fled, leaving Adria debating her duty.

"Let me go, sister. I beg of you."

Adria's grip didn't falter. "You hurt us. You hurt me. I stuck my neck out for you, and this is how you repay me? The humans are going to slaughter us, and now they know we're here. They'll hunt us until we're all dead."

"I don't believe that." I fought back tears. "Jack is a good man. Those humans are trying to save him. I want to save him. Please, let me go."

Adria glanced down at where the boss had disappeared, and I watched Jack drift away. Sobs pressed against my face. "You won't see me again, and I'll make sure the humans won't harm you. That's the best I can offer."

Adria's anger softened. Her eyes pinked with her own tears. "You're my sister. I wish things could be different, but you weren't meant for this work."

"You weren't meant for the boss's depravity, either. This isn't what I wanted, but I have to keep you safe, too. This is the only way I can do it. Let me go. Let me save him, and I'll make sure you're safe. I promise."

"I don't want to let you go," Adria said,

releasing me.

"I'll miss you," I said.

Adria nodded, and I turned away from her for the last time. Not concerned for my own safety, I swam to Jack, but a spear caught my arm—a flesh wound that drew blood. Ignoring it, I gripped Jack and rushed him to the surface.

Something was wrong.

Desperation

WITH MY POWERFUL TAIL fin, I kept us above the surface, bobbing over the gentle waves and keeping Jack's face in the air, but he didn't immediately cough or gasp. He wasn't moving at all. My chest constricted. "Jack, wake up." I squeezed his chest with a bear hug, hoping to rouse him or push the water out of his lungs. "Jack, please."

He didn't respond.

"Stay with me. I'm getting you help."

In the longboat, men leaned on steady feet and continued to launch spears down on their watery enemies. Their shouts of encouragement rang more afraid of the unknown than thirsty for the hunt. Regardless of their intentions when they saw me, they were my only hope.

I shouted, "Jack is here! He needs you!"

One sailor twisted to face me, spear tight

in his grasp and ready to launch, anger firmly in position on his youthful face. I held my breath. Please see reason, I silently begged. *Please don't be what the merfolk fear.*

After a beat, he assessed Jack's limp form. Rather than spear me as the cause of the man's condition, the sailor's anger gave way to concern, softening his face. He gestured. "Bring 'em here."

I exhaled and delivered Jack to the edge of the longboat, aware I was within catching distance myself, but so far, Jack had been right. The men made no indication they were a threat to me. "He's not breathing."

The humans pulled their drowned sailor aboard with a heavy *thud*, and I stayed at the rail. I couldn't leave. I had to know if they could revive him. I had to thank him for changing my life, for giving me the strength to break free from the chains of the Squad. Sobs pressed against my face as the men pounded on Jack's chest and uttered phrases of encouragement, but their efforts weren't working.

The remaining sailors continued their assault on the mermaids below, and as Jack wasn't improving, I dipped beneath the surface—not for the Squad's defense, but to make sure they wouldn't interfere again. All of the Salvage Squad had gone. Not knowing how many perished or escaped, I was free and Jack was safe...for now. I returned to the edge of the boat and hooked my arms over the rail to see. "Is he alive?"

The man pounding on Jack's chest reared back and gasped in surprise. I blinked. I didn't understand. "What is it? Why did you stop?"

Jack folded over to his side and retched up seawater. He took in a wet breath, and relief washed over me. I smiled as the men merrily patted him on the back and shoulders. Jack gestured his thanks and smiled. My heart swelled. He was going to be fine.

The man nearest to me grabbed my arm forcefully.

I frowned and tried to pull away.

"You're one of 'em, ain't you?" he said, eyes raking over me. "Very pretty, indeed."

Another man leaned over the rail, seeking the evidence below the surface. "Drag her aboard. She'll fetch a mighty prize."

Meaty hands heaved me over the rail, and I fell to the hull with a hip-bruising *thump*. The boat rocked, and the men circled me, maintaining their balance with ease. They marveled at me as if they'd never seen a mermaid this close before. Jack had promised these men would accept me, but the looks on their faces weren't kind or friendly. Not at all. Not anything like Jack's.

I tried to scoot back to the rail, but the uneven floor and tight edges gave me no leverage to haul myself back over. I was trapped. "Jack?" I whispered, cowering at the towering men around me.

The men parted and Jack reached out to me, shaking his head. "Leave her alone. She saved my life...twice." His gentle features for me lasted only a second.

"Despite her benevolent actions and our regard for you, we sustained injuries and deaths in that storm, and we must compensate the families of our lost souls. We all signed the articles, captain; we have no choice, and that's why we agreed to allow her on board," the man who'd gripped me said.

Captain Jack—*captain!*—climbed to his feet and stood between me and his men. "She's not for sale, and this isn't a negotiation. Don't make me tell you again."

The dissenter, a larger man in all ways, shifted closer to Jack with a stomach-curdling crease on his brow. "Tread carefully, captain. Disrespecting our dead leads to mutiny."

Jack didn't yield. "We will find another way. Leave her out of this."

"The biggest prize of our lives is right there." The dissenter pointed at me. "We will not give up that value."

Rage snarled Jack's fine features, and he dove at the bigger man. None of the crew interfered to support their captain. They only watched like cowards, unwilling to stand up for their boss against a dissenter. And here, moments ago, *I* was the dissenter. But I didn't need to master mathematics to be worried about Jack's odds.

As the scuffle progressed, the boat listed sharply, but the spectators maintained their balance with ease. As simple as a shove overboard would be Jack's end, because I wouldn't be able to escape to save him. I had to stop this now.

A Bargain

TRAPPED IN A BOAT with a useless floppy tail, I helplessly watched Jack fight in my honor against a more formidable dissenter. Jack's ivory tunic clung to his skin, revealing parts of him I wanted to see during a more happy moment. Damp hair whipped around his face, and boots slipped out from under him. The only way to stop them was to convince humans, who just learned of merfolk existence, that another treasure was far more valuable than me—the greatest treasure these men would ever discover. And an even bigger feat: they had to trust me. If I failed, I'd be sold all over again. The last time that happened didn't turn out so well, and I didn't imagine this time being any better. Even worse? Jack would go down fighting for me. I couldn't fail him—the one person who stood up for me. "I have something of greater value."

The men shifted their position and attention to me, and a lump formed in my throat. I was surrounded. From the bottom of the boat, they loomed large, intimidating, and fearless. The rocking of the boat slowed. Jack and the dissenter stopped their tussle, but I couldn't see the captain through these large men.

"More mermaids?" one man to my left asked. He was missing an eye, and I found it peculiar and distracting.

Jack stood on a bench, his head reaching above the others. He panted and looked upon me with worry on his brow. He was right to be concerned, but at least he would regain his strength with a short rest. If I had legs, I'd rush through these men to his side and hold on as if the world were about to tear us apart one final time.

I could do this. For him, I could do anything. "Better than that."

The men grinned in anticipation.

Nothing humans liked more than vast fortunes, and right now, that was my only leverage. "The Salvage Squad, that you so abruptly dispatched a moment ago, maintains a hoard of treasure from many sunken ships."

The dissenter shoved through the men, rocking the boat once more. "How can we trust your intelligence?"

The crew respected this intimidating man. If I could satisfy him, that might be all Jack and I needed. "Because I was one of them. I personally delivered gold, silver, and ivory, and I know exactly where it is. In exchange for my life, my freedom, I will collect it for you."

The men murmured, discussing the information. With my boss gone, those who survived the assault either required time to reorganize or they scattered for their freedom, too. A simple raid on their personal cache was a risk I'd happily take to preserve Jack's leadership and my life.

"So you're loyal to them," the man with the missing eye said skeptically. "If we let you go, you'll swim back to them."

Others murmured and nodded in agreement with him. That was not the response I expected.

"I won't. I swear," I pleaded. "I promise the value of the treasure—*years and years'* worth of collected treasure from dozens of ships—far exceeds anything you'd get for selling me. You won't regret it."

The dissenter considered my proposal, eyeing me cautiously. "How can we trust you?"

I smiled warmly at Jack, heart soaring with this new foreign feeling. "The same way I trusted you. By the word of a kind soul."

Jack's bright green eyes crinkled with affection in return, and he unbuttoned his damp tunic. Wanting to see what hid beneath the clingy fabric, heat flashed through my body. I didn't care that my heart was clear for all to see. Jack treated me better than my own family, my own sisters. I no longer needed to hide who I was. I was Calista, a rejected mermaid shifter in love with an extraordinary human.

Jack pushed through the men and peeled the ivory fabric off his shoulders, revealing a form and strength wrought by sun and hard labor. He was trim, dusted with dark hair, and I wanted to explore the curvature of his muscles. When his lips had touched my knuckles, an exciting feeling tore through me. I wanted that again. I wanted to touch my lips to his body and see where he took me.

Happily Ever After

As I stared in marvel at Jack's gorgeous, sculpted body, the men looked to their captain for a response, as if they'd decided to trust Jack's judgment again.

"She'll come back," Jack said, gesturing for me to approach him with his tunic in his hand. "And that's enough for me."

I wanted to feel his powerful arms curled around me. I wanted to touch that magnificent body of his, but my tail forbade me from standing. "I can't."

Jack's features twisted with increasing frustration at the men gawking at me, and Jack moved quickly around them, rocking the boat. He stumbled in close enough to kiss.

"What's wrong?" I whispered. I thought the bribe was going well.

Jack smiled and covered me with his tunic. It clung to my body and smelled of the salty sea—familiar, but also different. "Something's are best left to private chambers."

I cocked my head. While the fight had progressed, I had dried. My legs returned, and I was exposed. No wonder the men were gawking. Human men weren't much different from mermen. I sighed.

Jack helped me to my feet, and he embraced me. At last, the warm, strong arms held me close, and I never wanted him to let go. While the men listened, he said, "Thank you, fair maiden of the sea. You have given me a second chance at life, and I shall not waste it. Meeting you, however unfortunate the circumstances, has been the greatest thing to ever happen to me. Not all the gold in the world could compare, not the sunset on a Caribbean island, not a letter of pardon from the Governor. You are my treasure, and I love you. I want you by my side as we sail off into the horizon, hunting those invaluable treasures for these men. And when they're satisfied, we shall be free to explore the lands."

I exhaled deeply. Captain Jack Roberts would show me the depths of the world I could only dream, a real-life fairy tale, and he loved me. "That sounds perfect."

"Then I have another proposal for you," he added.

I nodded, waiting. The men snickered and murmured to each other. With a frown, Jack gestured a command to them, and they took up positions along the perimeter of the boat. Oars lifted. A man at the bow recited a word, and the oars struck the water with synchronicity. We glided closer to his vessel.

Jack leaned back and collected my hands in his. His brilliant green eyes met mine. "Calista, will you be my wife?"

I didn't need but a moment for the answer to come to me. I'd never been happier than at this moment, and I didn't make the handsome human wait for an answer. With a beaming grin that hurt my cheeks, I said eagerly, "I will. I love you, Jack."

The captain grinned and brushed frizzy dry hair away from my face. He focused on my lips. "Would you mind if I kissed you here, in front of my men, or do you want to wait until I can bring you into my chambers?"

I wanted him to kiss me. I couldn't wait for however long that would take. "Kiss me now."

While standing in a boat gliding over gentle waves toward the surviving ship in the cove,

Jack wrapped his arms around me, and I buried my hand in his hair and felt the strength of his back beneath my fingers. I wanted more. I wanted all of him. Jack's nose touched mine as he slowly closed the distance. Unable to wait any longer, I leaned forward, and my lips finally found his—soft, warm, and inviting. In that moment, he once more proved to me how much he cared. Jack wasn't ashamed of me or worried about his crew's opinions. They respected his order; they trusted my bribe, and while they rowed, they respectfully kept their eyes to their task.

As my lips learned his, my hands moved along his body, exploring his curves as new sensations accumulated down low. I couldn't wait for his chambers to kiss him, but I could wait for what lied beneath the rest of his clothing. Reluctantly, I pulled back. Jack's green eyes sparkled. "Jack?" I whispered.

"Yes?" he murmured between kisses.

"Do we have to set sail immediately, or can we have time alone?"

Jack's grin creased the corners of his beautiful eyes. "We will take all the time you want, my love."

I smiled and brought my lips back to his. I

couldn't get enough of him. Not only would I explore the depths of his body, but he would show me the depths of the world I'd always dreamed of. His fallen friends had not died in vain.

The sun broke through gray clouds, sending rays spotlighting the dark water. A new day had arrived. A new life had begun in the arms of my captain.

The End

Dear Reader,

As an indie author, I'm thrilled you shared your time with me, exploring the crazy worlds and voices living rent-free in my head and keeping me up at night. Your reviews are very important to me, so if you enjoyed this book, please consider leaving some stars at your favorite retailer for Calista and Jack's story, Depths of the Heart.

If you found any typos or errors, I blame my cat. Rat her out at: support@stephanieflynn.com.

Thank you for your support!

Also By Stephanie Flynn

Find my catalog at StephanieFlynn.com

Immortal Protector series

0.5 Vampire's Distraction

1 Vampire's Deception

2 Vampire's Secret

3 Vampire's Promise

3.5 Elf Bound

4 Vampire's Demand

5 Vampire's Destruction

6 Vampire's Conquest

Immortal Protector Side Tales

Deer Holiday

Love Claws
Depths of the Heart

Matchmaker in Time series
0.5 Minutes to Live
1 Seconds to Act
2 Hours to Arrive
3 Days to Hide
4 Years to Savor

Pirates in Time series
1 Pirate's Prize
2 Pirate's Treasure
3 Pirate's Plunder

Time Travel Romance Shorts
Fateful Time
One Crazy Time

If you like your urban fantasy without the romance, too, check out Stephanie Flynn's other name, Marie Flynn!

About Stephanie Flynn

Stephanie Flynn writes action-packed paranormal romance filled with adventure, suspense, and danger. She lives in Michigan, USA, with her husband and kids, and she spends her writing time surrounded by a herd of normal cats who bat everything off her desk, including her coffee. Check out her website for more books: StephanieFlynn.com

www.ingramcontent.com/pod-product-compliance
Lightning Source LLC
Chambersburg PA
CBHW031419200726
48285CB00017BA/2552